Rabbit and Robot

by Liza Charlesworth

ISBN: 978-1-338-89037-2

Designer: Cynthia Ng; Illustrated by John Lund

1 2 3 4 5 6 7 8 9 10 68 31 30 29 28 27 26 25 24 23 22

Printed in Jiaxing, China. First printing, January 2023.

This is a story about a toy named Rabbit.
Rabbit was chatty and stuffed with fluff.
He always went VERY fast.
Hop, hop, hop!

This is a story about a toy named Robot.
Robot was shy and made of metal.
He always went VERY slow.
Clank, clank, clank!

3

Rabbit and Robot lived in Toyland,
and they were best friends.
Robot liked Rabbit except for one thing:
Rabbit bragged A LOT, LOT, LOT!
"I'm great at being a pal!" bragged Rabbit.

"I'm also great at reading books!
I'm also great at drawing pictures!
I'm also the fastest toy
in all the land!"

5

Then, Rabbit said to Robot,
"Let's have a race so I can prove it."
"OK," replied Robot. "I am NOT fast,
but I will try my VERY best."
So the friends went to the starting line.
"ONE, TWO, THREE, GO!" roared Dinosaur.

Rabbit took off like a flash.
He was fast. *Hop, hop, hop!*
Robot was slow. *Clank, clank, clank!*
But he did try his VERY best.

Hop, hop, hop! Clank, clank, clank!
After a while, Rabbit was WAY ahead of Robot.
So he decided to take a break
under a shady apple tree.
What did Rabbit do during his break?

He talked on his cell phone.
Chat, chat, chat.

He drew a pretty picture.
Draw, draw, draw.

He ate three big apples.
Crunch, crunch, crunch!

He read an awesome folktale.
Read, read, read.

But reading the book
made Rabbit feel tired.
So he fell fast asleep
and began to dream.
Zzzzzzzzzzzzzzzzzzzzzzzzzzzzzz!

What did Robot do while Rabbit dreamed?
He kept going. *Clank, clank, clank!*
Robot was NOT fast, but he didn't give up.
As Rabbit slept on, Robot got closer
and closer to the finish line.

BONK!
Just then, an apple fell from the tree
and hit Rabbit on the head.
Rabbit opened up his eyes.
"OH, NO!" he screamed.
"Robot is in the lead!"

So Rabbit jumped up
and got back on the path.
Rabbit went fast. *Hop, hop, hop!*
Robot went slow. *Clank, clank, clank!*
Could Rabbit beat Robot?

NOPE!
Rabbit was a bit too late.
Robot reached the finish line first
and won the race!
All the toys cheered...

...even Rabbit, who was proud of his pal.
"I learned my lesson," he declared.
"I will never brag again except to say:
I have the GREATEST friend
in all of Toyland!"